SHIVER me TIMBERS!

Pirate Poems
& Paintings

poems by
DOUGLAS FLORIAN

pirates by
ROBERT NEUBECKER

BEACH LANE BOOKS

new york   london   toronto   sydney   new delhi

Pirates Wear Patches

Pirates wear patches.
Pirates have hooks.
They all play with matches
And give dirty looks.

Pirates wear white shirts
With big puffy sleeves.
Pirates are scoundrels
And rascals and thieves.

Pirates wear tricornes
Of felt with a feather.
Pirates are known to cause
Inclement weather.

Pirates wear long scraggly
Beards on their chins.
Pirates wear smirks
With immense evil grins.

Pirates have parrots
And eat alligator.
Pirates shoot first
And then ask questions later.

Pirate Patter

Ahoy, matey means Hello, my friend.

Heave to means come to an end.

A cat-o'-nine-tails is a whip.

A man-o'-war is a sailing ship.

The Jolly Roger is the pirates' flag.

A villainous person is a scallywag.

A pirates' drink is called a grog.

A rotten pirate is a scurvy dog.

Aye means Yes, I do agree.

Davy Jones's locker is the bottom of the sea.

Feed the fish means throw overboard.

A cutlass is a short, curved sword.

Pillage means to raid or seize.

There is no pirate word for please.

The Pirates' Code of Conduct

Don't take a bath.

Avoid all math.

It's best to yell

And blessed to smell.

Act rash and rude.

Dash down yer food.

Be sure to slurp

And belch and burp.

Take lots of naps.

Hide all yer maps.

Dismay, disrupt,

And interrupt.

Rob, steal, and loot,

But don't get cute.

Tell lots of lies.

Make alibis.

Don't change yer clothes.

Yell, "Thar she blows!"

Names for Pirates

Pirates, picaroons, buccaneers.

Freebooters, filibusters, privateers.

Raiders, rovers, salt sea-robbers.

Avast ye lily-livered landlubbers!

Pirate Punishment

They put me in an iron cage,
Then made me walk the plank.
They tied me legs in heavy chains
After they stole me rank.

For weeks on end they made me spend
Dark days inside a dungeon,
Then carried me
Out to the sea
And ordered me to plunge in.

They tried to hang me seven times.
Ten times they broke me knees.
But worst of all
They had the gall
To make me eat me peas!

Hiring Pirates

Hiring pirates: to sail to all nations.
Hiring pirates: without paid vacations.

Hiring pirates: must know to rig sails.
Hiring pirates: and be hard as nails.

Hiring pirates: required to scare.
Hiring pirates: and frequently swear.

Hiring pirates: familiar with knots.
Hiring pirates: who have all their shots.

Hiring pirates: to set sail due east.
Hiring pirates: man, woman, or beast.

Pirates' Meal

On Monday we had haddock.

On Tuesday tuna fish.

We dined on weakfish Wednesday.

Shark, our Thursday dish.

On Friday we had flounder.

Saturday ate fluke.

If we have fish for one more day

Methinks that I will puke.

Blackbeard

Blackbeard braided his long black beard,
Then tied the braids with bows.
He stuffed burning rope beneath his hat.
Put a ring right through his nose.

Blackbeard boarded many a ship
To pillage and plunder and steal.
He robbed with pleasure
Great troves of treasure,
Which he did his best to conceal.

Blackbeard feared no other man—
A pirate as cruel as they come.
One look from his eyes
Could terrorize,
But he always wrote home to his mum.

Buried Treasure

When I was young
I sailed among
Some pirates out at sea.
They were a ruthless, toothless lot,
As nasty as could be.
One day we swarmed a treasure ship,
And captured all thar gold
Along with rubies, brilliant red,
As much as we could hold;

Green emeralds and malachite;
Blue sapphire jewels and more.
We put them all into a chest
And carried it ashore
To bury deep beneath the sand.
A big X marked the spot.
A buried treasure in the sand—
But just whar?
I forgot!

But never-
the-
less,

Despite

all

me

mess,

I am a movie starrr!

Me, Pirate

Me nose is long.
Me ears look wrong.
Me face makes children cry.
Me scraggly beard
Is very weird.
Me breath makes flowers die.

I am a brute.
Not one bit cute.
A really rotten egg.
I'm four feet high,
Missing one eye.
I have a wooden leg.

Me skin has moles.
Me teeth have holes.
I've gnarly, knobby knees.
Me voice is hoarse,
But what is worse,
Me foot smells like Swiss cheese.

I'm bony thin,
Ugly as sin.
I've got a six-inch scar.

Pirates Pirate

Some pirates pirate rubies.

Some pirates pirate gold.

Some pirates pirate diamonds:

All that thar hands can hold.

Some pirates pirate spices.

They steal without a care.

Some pirates pirate pirates—

Arrgh, matey, best beware!

Turtle Day

Turtle eggs for breakfast.
Turtle stew for lunch.
Turtle shell for dinner.
Crunch!
   Crunch!
      Crunch!

Captain Kidd

I'm Captain Kidd,

Me treasure is hid

In a chest on Gardiners Isle.

Beneath the ground

It can be found:

Gold coins (that's why I smile).

Been buried here

Fer many a year

Since 1669.

So if one day

It comes yer way,

Remember: It's all mine!

Pirate Flags

Heart pierced by a knife:
Best fear fer yer life!

Giant hourglass:
Yer life will now pass!

Two bones that are crossed:
All soon will be lost!

Skeleton's grinning head:
Thar's dread dead ahead!

Half a skeleton's head:
We ran out of white thread!

Me Pirate Weapons

A cutlass sword.

A boarding axe.

A pistol for surprise attacks.

A blunderbuss.

A straight-blade dagger.

A sulfur stinkpot makes 'em stagger.

Two tomahawks, both small in size.

Me scariest weapon?

It is me eyes.

Rule of the Pirate

Licensed pirate: privateer.

Ruthless pirate: buccaneer.

Aim of the pirate: commandeer.

Rule of the pirate: have no fear.

Pyrates

We're pyrates, tyrant pyrates,

And we sail the pyra-seas.

We raid and plunder treasure ships

To steal and pyra-seize.

We're rude, crude dudes with attitudes.

We're motley and we're mean.

We love to try to make you cry

And cause a pyra-scene.

ARR!
BOO!

Arrr!

We call our ship a man-o'-warrr!

We sail to ports both near and farrr!

From Timbuktu to Madagascarrr!

At night we navigate by starrr!

We're hard as nails with many a scarrr!

We're pirates, scary pirates we arrr!

A Pirate's Life

A pirate's life is topsy-turvy,

Full of strife, and rife with scurvy.

Pirates have to follow orders,

Sleep in dank, dark, dampest quarters.

Misbehave, you'll get the whip,

Or what's worse: thrown off the ship.

Moldy biscuits, rotten meats.

Don't expect no late-night treats.

Fights are settled by a duel.

No vacations, as a rule.

Days of boring life at sea—

A pirate's life is not fer me!

For my cousin Bob Solomons, of blessed memory
—D. F.

To Isabel Ruth Jean Lafitte
—R. N.

BEACH LANE BOOKS • An imprint of Simon & Schuster Children's Publishing Division • 1230 Avenue of the Americas, New York, New York 10020 • Text copyright © 2012 by Douglas Florian • Illustrations copyright © 2012 by Robert Neubecker • All rights reserved, including the right of reproduction in whole or in part in any form. • BEACH LANE BOOKS is a trademark of Simon & Schuster, Inc. • For information about special discounts for bulk purchases, please contact Simon & Schuster Special Sales at 1-866-506-1949 or business@simonandschuster.com. • The Simon & Schuster Speakers Bureau can bring authors to your live event. For more information or to book an event, contact the Simon & Schuster Speakers Bureau at 1-866-248-3049 or visit our website at www.simonspeakers.com. • Book design by Lauren Rille • The text for this book is set in Caslon Antique. • The illustrations for this book are rendered in India ink on watercolor paper and then colored digitally. • Manufactured in China • 0612 SCP • First Edition • 10 9 8 7 6 5 4 3 2 1 • Library of Congress Cataloging-in-Publication Data • Florian, Douglas. • Shiver me timbers / Douglas Florian ; illustrated by Robert Neubecker.—1st ed. • p. cm. • ISBN 978-1-4424-1321-4 • 1. Pirates—Juvenile poetry. 2. Children's poetry, American. I. Neubecker, Robert. II. Title. PS3556.L589S55 2012 • 811'.54—dc22 • 2010048963